Acting Edition

I0591754

How a Boy Falls

by Steven Dietz

FOR PRODUCTION INQUIRIES

UNITED STATES AND CANADA
info@concordtheatricals.com
1-866-979-0447

UNITED KINGDOM AND EUROPE
licensing@concordtheatricals.co.uk
020-7054-7298

Each title is subject to availability from Concord Theatricals Corp., depending upon country of performance. Please be aware that *HOW A BOY FALLS* may not be licensed by Concord Theatricals Corp. in your territory. Professional and amateur producers should contact the nearest Concord Theatricals Corp. office or licensing partner to verify availability.

No one shall make any changes in this title(s) for the purpose of production. No part of this book may be reproduced, stored in a retrieval system, scanned, uploaded, or transmitted in any form, by any means, now known or yet to be invented, including mechanical, electronic, digital, photocopying, recording, videotaping, or otherwise, without the prior written permission of the publisher. No one shall share this title(s), or any part of this title(s), through any social media or file hosting websites.

For all inquiries regarding motion picture, television, online/digital and other media rights, please contact Concord Theatricals Corp.

MUSIC AND THIRD-PARTY MATERIALS USE NOTE

Licensees are solely responsible for obtaining formal written permission from copyright owners to use copyrighted music and/or other copyrighted third-party materials (e.g. artworks, logos) in the performance of this play and are strongly cautioned to do so. If no such permission is obtained by the licensee, then the licensee must use only original music and materials that the licensee owns and controls. Licensees are solely responsible and liable for clearances of all third-party copyrighted materials, including without limitation music, and shall indemnify the copyright owners of the play(s) and their licensing agent, Concord Theatricals Corp., against any costs, expenses, losses and liabilities arising from the use of such copyrighted third-party materials by licensees. For music, please contact the appropriate music licensing authority in your territory for the rights to any incidental music.

IMPORTANT BILLING AND CREDIT REQUIREMENTS

If you have obtained performance rights to this title, please refer to your licensing agreement for important billing and credit requirements.

HOW A BOY FALLS received its world premiere at Northlight Theatre (BJ Jones, Artistic Director, Timothy J. Evans, Managing Director) in Evanston, IL, on January 31st, 2020. The production was directed by Halena Kays, scenic design by Lizzie Bracken, costume design by Izumi Inaba, lighting design by Jason Lynch, sound design by Rick Sims, the dramaturg was Tanya Palmer, and the stage manager was Rita Vreeland. The cast was as follows:

CHELLE.................................Cassidy Slaughter-Mason
SAM... Sean Parris
PAUL...Tim Decker
MIRANDA.. Michelle Duffy
MITCH...Travis A. Knight

This play received developmental support from PlayPenn, Philadelphia, PA, Paul Meshejian, Artistic Director.

CHARACTERS

CHELLE – a woman, twenty-nine.

SAM – a man, thirty.

PAUL – a man, fifty-two.

MIRANDA – a woman, fifty.

MITCH – a man, thirty-five.

SETTING

An American city on the water.

And a town on the Mediterranean.

TIME

The present.

AUTHOR'S NOTES

What's on stage:

It is spare, clean and nimble. A table, a bench, and some chairs should serve to transform the space. The few, specific items called for (such as the flowers) should feel significant against the simplicity of the environment. Also: some indication of a balcony railing would be welcome.

How it moves:

In most every case, these scenes happen "out" of one another rather than "after" one another. Any chance to have a character walk directly from one scene/setting to the next should be exploited. There are no transitional moments required or intended. There is also no need to depict "passage of time" – forward or back – or to indicate to the audience if a scene takes place "*Now*" or "*Then*."

for BJ Jones

1.

(*Now.*)

(**CHELLE** *sits, waiting, at a small table in a coffee shop. She holds a takeaway coffee. A second chair at the table is empty.*)

(**SAM** *is standing nearby, staring at* **CHELLE**. **MITCH** *is standing near* **SAM**. *They do not know each other.*)

(**CHELLE** *cannot see or hear either of the men.*)

MITCH. (*Friendly, upbeat.*) Do you know her?

SAM. Huh?

MITCH. This woman you are staring at.

SAM. Oh. No. No, I don't.

And I wasn't staring. I was just.

(*Beat.* **MITCH** *smiles.*)

MITCH. Yeah. Right.

(**SAM** *and* **MITCH** *both watch* **CHELLE**.)

She comes in a lot. Usually takes her coffee and goes. Not today, though.

(*They watch* **CHELLE** *some more.*)

I don't know her name. Wish I did. Never had the nerve.

(**SAM** *nods. He tries – without success – not to stare at* **CHELLE**.)

MITCH. First time in here?

SAM. What? – oh, yeah.

MITCH. Pretty good place. Live nearby?

SAM. I did. I used to.

MITCH. Been awhile?

SAM. Yeah.

MITCH. Where were you before?

SAM. I was out in the Bay Area.

MITCH. Nice. Something brought you back?

(*Off* **SAM**'s *look.*)

I ask a lot of questions. Occupational hazard. I'm sorry...

(**MITCH** *leans in, fishing for* **SAM**'s *name...*)

SAM. ...Sam.

MITCH. Good to meet you, Sam.

(*Shaking hands.*)

Mike Mitchell. Folks call me Mitch. How's it goin'?

SAM. Oh, you know – it's.

MITCH. Livin' the dream, right? Back in the old neighborhood. Maybe just comin' off a move. Or a job change. Something big. Maybe a break-up.

(*Off* **SAM**'s *look.*)

You just have that look.

SAM. What look?

> (**MITCH** *smiles, shrugs, sips his coffee.*)

I'm just coming off a move.

MITCH. Okay.

SAM. After a breakup.

How'd you know that?

MITCH. *(Lightly.)* I don't know, Sam. How do I know anything?

SAM. She was a lovely woman. Smart and funny. Lot of shared interests.

MITCH. I don't like where this is going –

SAM. She said she couldn't see a future with me.

MITCH. Ouch.

SAM. "You're too cautious." – those were her words. "You *look*, Sam – but you won't ever *leap*." Said she needed someone a little more "reckless." With a little more "abandon."

MITCH. Wow. Reminds me of this woman in Philly. She was an architect. Big fan of punk music. Had these great tattoos. I'm trying not to embarrass myself at the bar – I'm sayin' the two things I know about the Ramones over and over again – and pretty soon she is giving me the code to her building:

Star – seven – three – fifty-six – forty-nine.

SAM. You still remember the code?

MITCH. Of course I do. *Never forget the code.* And oh man, I could have made something happen there.

But I was like you.

Too cautious.

MITCH. And she was gone.

Thresholds, Sam.

SAM. Hmm?

MITCH. Threshold moments.

We either back away.

Or we step across.

> *(Looking at* **CHELLE.***)*

Like this woman we are both not staring at.

I'm in security, Sam. People think it's all gadgets and technology. But most of it is people. Reading people.

> *(Looking at* **CHELLE.***)*

Extra chair at the table.

Checking the time.

Looking over her shoulder.

This woman is not hard to read.

This woman is waiting for someone.

Maybe one of us could be the person she is waiting for.

SAM. *(With a laugh.)* Yeah, right – I gotta go –

MITCH. Here's the thing:

We might walk up.

We might say as little as possible.

And we might *follow her lead.*

There is always someone they want us to be –

SAM. C'mon – that's not –

MITCH. – so why can't you *be that guy?*

SAM. Me?

(**SAM** *is looking at* **CHELLE**, *considering...*)

MITCH. Oh, I forgot. Sam *looks* – but he doesn't *leap*.

(**CHELLE** *stands. She gathers up her things, preparing to leave.*)

And away she goes.

SAM. No...

MITCH. *Thresholds, Sam.*

SAM. I'm not doing this...

(**CHELLE** *turns to go.*)

MITCH. We either back away.

Or we step across.

(*And* **SAM** *suddenly walks toward* **CHELLE**, *as –*)

2.

(Then.)

*(– **PAUL** approaches **CHELLE** from another direction. Same coffee shop. **PAUL** wears a nice suit.)*

PAUL. Are you Michelle?

*(**CHELLE** stops. Turns to him.)*

I'm so sorry. I had cleared my meetings for the afternoon – but just as I was leaving the office –

(Stops, restarts.)

It doesn't matter. I'm sorry to be late.

Paul.

We spoke on the phone.

(They shake hands.)

CHELLE. *(Pronounced "ron-DEEN.")* You're Mr. Rondine?

PAUL. You thought you were meeting with my wife.

CHELLE. Yes.

PAUL. Miranda. You'll love Miranda. But she couldn't get away. Alex had a dentist appointment, and –

CHELLE. Your son, Alex.

PAUL. Yes.

CHELLE. He's four.

PAUL. Very good! You've done your homework on us. I call him Alex, but his mother is determined to raise him as an Alexander. Names matter, of course. But – still – this friendly disagreement is something you should know about us if you're going to work as our *au pair.*

CHELLE. I thought an *au pair* was from a foreign country.

PAUL. Where are you from?

CHELLE. Cincinnati.

PAUL. *(Lightly.)* Well – Cincinnati is foreign to me. Can't an *au pair* be from Cincinnati?

CHELLE. The agency said you were looking for a "nanny."

PAUL. And here we are back at names again! But, if it's all the same to you, Michelle – I'd like to think of you as our *au pair*. May we do that?

> (**CHELLE** *is staring at him.*)

You expected an interview.

CHELLE. Well…

PAUL. I'm sorry. My wife would know how to do this. Miranda would have a million questions for you.

CHELLE. It's okay, you don't –

PAUL. No, please, tell me: how should we do this? I want to do this right.

> (**CHELLE** *removes a professional-looking folder from her bag.*)

CHELLE. Here is my resumé. You'll see my education and experience. The other families I've worked for. Letters of recommendation.

> (**PAUL** *is looking at the papers in the folder, with interest.*)

Is something wrong?

PAUL. *(From the resumé.)* You studied Camus. In school. The literature of the existentialists.

CHELLE. Guilty as charged.

PAUL. Camus. Sartre. Simone de Beauvoir.

CHELLE. *(With a smile.)* All of which prepared me for a career as a nanny.

> *(**CHELLE** expects at least a smile. Instead, **PAUL** says:)*

PAUL. *"There is no country for those who despair. But I know that the sea comes before and after me, and hold my madness ready."*

> *(**PAUL** looks to her...)*

CHELLE. Camus. *The Sea Close By.*

PAUL. Have you ever seen the Mediterranean?

CHELLE. No.

PAUL. It is exactly as Camus describes it.

The blue of that water.

The heat of that sun.

When I first met my wife, she had on a dress of Mediterranean blue. We caught each other's eye in the lobby of the Fairmont Hotel. And on a table behind her was a vase of flowers...perfect yellow daffodils.

My life – quite literally – began at that moment. The moment I met Miranda.

> *(A warm smile.)*

Do you have moments like that?

Moments you just can't shake?

CHELLE. *(Beat, quietly.)* Yes.

PAUL. You have the address of the house? Miranda's phone and mine?

CHELLE. Yes.

PAUL. *(The papers.)* And may I keep these?

CHELLE. Yes. Of course. But –

PAUL. People try to tell you how it will feel – when you have a child of your own. Someone will hand you their baby and say "isn't it amazing?" – and it is, of course. But holding someone else's child is nothing at all like holding your own.

When I look at Alex...when I kiss his sweet, sweaty head...when I imagine him in danger, imagine any harm coming to him...the feeling I get, Michelle:

It is feral.

It is fierce and irrational.

And I know I would do *anything at all in this world* to ensure his safety.

I will expect you to do the same.

>   (**PAUL** *turns and leaves, as –*)

3.

(Then.)

*(– **MIRANDA** appears, nicely dressed, in her home. She sets a vase of perfect yellow daffodils in the room.)*

MIRANDA. *(Cordial, poised.)* I've never cared for this house. But Paul – he likes the prestige of it. Even the address embarrasses me. One Paragon Lane. I mean, really.

CHELLE. But the view...it's breathtaking.

MIRANDA. Paul talks about a book in which a group of friends live in a "House Above the World."

CHELLE. That's Camus.

MIRANDA. I think that's the feeling Paul wanted, when we built this. He loves to show people the view.

But all I see is the fall.

The far balcony – facing west – that balcony is cantilevered well out over the ocean. Paul assures me it's all to code. The height of the railing. The vertical slats beneath. He says nothing could get between those slats. I checked anyway. Measured it myself. I called the sheriff in the closest town – asked him the response time, in case of emergency.

Because there is no good way to access that cove from below. *That drop,* Michelle – my fear of that drop – that is what I see when you and all the others see "the view."

(Beat.)

CHELLE. *(Pronounced "SHELL.")* I'm called Chelle. It's a nickname. But I prefer it.

MIRANDA. Chelle. Yes. Thank you. Names matter.

CHELLE. Yes, that's what your –

MIRANDA. How old are you?

CHELLE. Twenty-four.

MIRANDA. And still doing this? Babysitting.

CHELLE. Your husband called it an *au pair.*

MIRANDA. *(Lightly.)* I'm sure he did. And the position that was listed – was it a "live-in" situation?

CHELLE. Yes – live-in. A live-in nanny.

MIRANDA. *(With a smile.)* And you'd want that? You'd want to live with people like us?

CHELLE. Well –

MIRANDA. Don't get me wrong. We have our good days. And then we have our days when, apparently, we are interviewing a nanny. When apparently someone is going to come live in our home.

(Beat.)

CHELLE. You didn't know?

*(**MIRANDA** just stares at her.)*

He said you ran the listing. Your husband said –

MIRANDA. Yes, I know he did.

And here we are.

CHELLE. Oh, god – I'm so sorry – I thought –

(Stops.)

I had no idea.

MIRANDA. What else did Paul say?

CHELLE. He said you'd have a million questions.

MIRANDA. Oh, I do. I really do.

Let me guess. You're looking to make a fresh start. New city. New job. New haircut?

CHELLE. Well – sort of –

MIRANDA. Oh – I envy you a new start. At my age, I don't think it's in the cards, anymore. You, however! – you're still young (though you're not twenty-four, I don't think) – you still have so much time to make it right. *(Before* **CHELLE** *can respond.)* And you can't hear that – not yet. Back when I was your age (twenty-nine? – maybe closer to thirty?) – back then, no one could tell me anything.

CHELLE. He told me how you met.

He said you had on a dress of Mediterranean blue.

And his face just...lit up. I've never had anyone do that...have their face just *light up* when they talked about me.

MIRANDA. That was nearly ten years ago...seems impossible...but we have an anniversary coming up. It was all such a whirlwind. One of those times in your life when everything is a "sign."

I remember I was staying in room two oh five – and I was sure it was a "sign" that the number of Paul's room was the exact opposite of mine. God, to feel so young.

Three weeks later – to the day – we were married.

CHELLE. Your first?

MIRANDA. Yes. I married late.

CHELLE. And Paul?

MIRANDA. His past – his life before meeting me...I know very little about it. It didn't matter.

CHELLE. He says his life began with you.

(Beat.)

MIRANDA. You don't miss a thing, do you?

CHELLE. But why do you stay?

(Off **MIRANDA***'s look.)*

I mean: in the house. If you don't care for it –

MIRANDA. I stay because I have a boy.

Born to me late in life.

My beautiful Alexander.

(Candid.) And the rest of what I wanted?

Well – hey: most of that has fallen away.

> (**MIRANDA** *is gathering up her purse and car keys.*)

It was nice to meet you, Chelle. But we don't need a nanny. I look after my son and I don't need –

CHELLE. *(Suddenly, with force.)* My mother got sick. I left school to care for her. It was terrible. She lost it all. Her house, her savings – everything –

MIRANDA. I'm sorry...

CHELLE. *(Continuous.)* – *Do you know what ovarian cancer does to someone? Do you know how it just guts them like they were a fish?* Till there's nothing left at all. Just...paperwork. Ashes. Debts.

(Desperately.) Make a job for me. *Please.*

If not as a nanny – anything. I will clean – do laundry, yard work – *anything.*

MIRANDA. Did you tell my husband that? That you'd do anything?

CHELLE. No.

(Pause.)

MIRANDA. I'm sorry about your mother. How old was she?

CHELLE. Your age.

(*Beat.*)

MIRANDA. Which is?

CHELLE. Fifty.

Ish.

(*A hint of a smile from* **MIRANDA**.)

MIRANDA. Alexander loves Hide-N-Seek. He could play it all day. And we count in different languages – just for fun. First in English, then in Spanish, then in French –

CHELLE. I don't know any French.

MIRANDA. I don't either. I'm learning.

CHELLE. And does he always hide in the exact same place?

MIRANDA. Yes! He usually does. How did you –?

CHELLE. Kids do that. I don't know why.

(*Beat.*)

MIRANDA. Come tomorrow at noon. We'll see how it goes.

(**MIRANDA** *goes, as –*)

4.

(Now. Continuous from Scene 1.)

*(– **CHELLE** gathers up her things, preparing to leave –)*

MITCH. *Thresholds, Sam.*

SAM. I'm not doing this...

*(**CHELLE** turns to go.)*

MITCH. We either back away.

Or we step across.

*(Suddenly, **SAM** walks toward the table, intercepting **CHELLE** –)*

SAM. Hi there.

*(**CHELLE** stares at him, hard.)*

You've been waiting.

CHELLE. *(Sharp, urgent.)* Where've you been?! Your text said three. *It's after four.*

SAM. Yeah – I'm sorry – there was a thing.

CHELLE. We can't talk here, anyway. I don't know why I agreed to meet here.

SAM. No – neither do I.

CHELLE. It was *your* idea! I thought you knew how to do this. Jesus – did I? – are you not –? Oh, god...

SAM. No – listen – we can do this somewhere else –

CHELLE. I'm Chelle. That's my real name, by the way. I know you can't use yours. I'll call you "Rick" – like you asked me to. I get why you can't use your real name – but are you – I mean – *just to make sure:*

CHELLE. *We've been texting, right? This past week? You and me?* You wouldn't send a photo. And there was nothing online about you at all. *But you're Rick, right?* I mean, like: "Rick." The guys at the gym gave me your number. Maybe they told you about me.

I'm Chelle.

> (*A moment of uncertainty...then:* **SAM** *extends his hand.*)

SAM. *Rick.* Good to meet you.

CHELLE. You've done this before?

SAM. Oh, sure.

CHELLE. And you're good at it? I mean...no one has found you out?

> (*Beat.*)

SAM. (*A tense smile.*) I'm here, aren't I?

CHELLE. I was texting you just now. Why didn't you respond?

SAM. Oh – I had to change my number.

CHELLE. Okay. That makes sense. I guess you'd have to do that. I called you on a "burner" – a burner phone.

SAM. That's cool –

CHELLE. Can't be traced.

SAM. – I've heard about those.

CHELLE. I had to get one. You should give me your new number, when you get it. I mean, if we decide to go through with this.

> (*Off* **SAM***'s look.*)

There's a bench – at the park down the street. We can talk there.

SAM. Sounds good.

CHELLE. But we should walk separately.

SAM. Separately?

CHELLE. Well – I mean – *obviously.*

> *(Suddenly.)* It's bad. Maybe the guys at the gym told you. It's bad and I don't know what to do. I found a suitcase that he was hiding at the house, and I think –

> *(Stops, off* **SAM***'s stare.)*

What do you care, right? – you probably just want your money. And I can get you the money. I've taken care of that.

SAM. Oh, okay – but that's not –

CHELLE. I really thought they were kidding – the guys at the gym – Pablo and Skip – I thought they were just talking their bullshit – you probably know how they love to talk their bullshit –

SAM. Yeah, right –

CHELLE. – but I can promise you the last thing I thought they'd say was:

"You know, Chelle – *you can have someone killed.*"

"There are people who do that for people. Like this guy Rick we know."

I laughed in their face. But the next day, Pablo slipped me a note with your number on it. He said you could make it look like an accident. Is that true?

> *(***SAM*** is staring at her, blankly.)*

CHELLE. *(Whispers.)* I can't believe I'm here and we are talking about this.

Can you believe we are talking about this?

SAM. No, I can't.

CHELLE. *(Leans in.)* So...how would you do it?

     (Beat.)

SAM. We shouldn't discuss this here.

CHELLE. Okay, right. The park. See you there.

     (**CHELLE** *walks away and is gone.*)

     (**MITCH** *appears. He has watched – but not heard – the conversation.*)

MITCH. Wow, Sammy! Way to take the leap!

SAM. I just did what you said. Tried to be who she wanted –

MITCH. That's great.

So, who does she think you are?

5.

(Then.)

(CHELLE sits, outdoors, on a park bench. Her eyes are red. She is fixated on something high above, at some distance in front of her.)

(After a moment, PAUL appears.)

PAUL. It's not good for you. To sit and stare at it. It won't change anything. There will no charges filed until –

(Stops, pause.)

As the officer said – "until such time as the body is found."

Miranda knows him. This sheriff. He's from the town just down the coast. She's been talking to him about the search. But this young sheriff...he's not hopeful. The rocks, the waves in the cove. The undertow.

She knows, by the way.

Miranda knows that it was your fault.

Your negligence.

Have you seen her, yet?

(CHELLE shakes her head "no.")

God help you when you do.

And whatever this is – *whatever performance you are giving here* – looking up at that balcony will not bring my boy back.

(PAUL seems to be finished talking with her.)

(CHELLE slowly stands and prepares to leave. When she does so –)

PAUL. *I trusted you.*

I trusted you with my son.

Miranda said "Why should we file charges against her? – it won't bring Alexander back."

I said: we file charges to *punish her*.

To make her *know* – to make *you* know what you *did to us*.

This should haunt you.

This should fucking *haunt* you.

You should not get to move on – you should not get your life back – you should not get to do anything but *ache*, you fraud, you fucking *fake*.

> (**PAUL** *leaves, as –*)

> (**CHELLE** *immediately calls after him:*)

CHELLE.   I'm sorry! I'm SO SORRY! PLEASE! – MR. RONDINE! – *I'LL DO ANYTHING –*

> (**CHELLE** *stares in the direction* **PAUL** *left for a long time. And then...*)

> (**CHELLE** *sits once again. She takes a deep breath. She takes one final look up at the balcony, as –*)

6.

(Now.)

*(– **SAM** arrives at the park bench. He is holding Chelle's takeaway coffee cup.)*

*(**CHELLE** does not turn to him.)*

CHELLE. Hi, Rick.

SAM. Hey.

You left your coffee. I thought...

I thought you might want your coffee.

CHELLE. Sorry. My mind is wandering. That's not good. I bet you don't do that. I bet you *compartmentalize*, right? I wish I could.

You and me, Rick...god...We're both killers.

That should be funny.

That should be a funny thing to say.

Why couldn't I have been there?

Why couldn't I have stopped him?

SAM. Stopped who?

(She turns to him.)

CHELLE. Are you going to sit down?

*(**SAM** sits on the bench with her. He hands her the coffee.)*

I was his nanny.

He was four.

His dad – Mr. Rondine – was at home.

CHELLE. His mom was out for the day.

And Alex – Alexander – wanted to play Hide-N-Seek.

We were in the kitchen. Alex had on his Mickey Mouse cap – the black felt one, with the little ears. He said "Ready-Set-Go" – and he ran off to hide.

I heard him running around the house – but I knew he'd end up in the entryway closet, hiding behind the coats. That's always where he went.

When I got to fifty, I opened my eyes and shouted: *"Ready or Not – here I come!"*

I saw that the door to the balcony was open. I started to rush out – but right then my phone rang.

I shouldn't have answered it.

If I had ignored that call, none of this would've –

(Stops, beat.)

It was loud on the balcony. Always very loud – because of the waves and the rocks below. I looked around – playing the game – I kept saying *"Aaaaalex...where aaaaare you?!"* – waiting to hear him giggle. He always giggled a little right before I found him.

I happened to look over the balcony railing.

And that's when I saw his Mickey Mouse cap.

It was down by the rocks.

Floating in the water.

I called for him – looked everywhere on the balcony – and then I was screaming – the dad came running out. *I told him Alex must have fallen. I told him it was my fault.*

And Mr. Rondine panicked – he grabbed me – started shaking me – he raced down the stairs at the side of the balcony – I followed but I couldn't keep up – he was calling *AAAAAALLEX!* – and he ran down to the water – climbed out onto the rocks – *trying to find his son.*

Two full weeks, the police searched. Used patrol boats. Helicopters. Divers.

They found that Mickey Mouse cap.
A little blue tennis shoe.
Part of a T-shirt.

That was all.

>   *(Silence.)*

SAM. When was this?

CHELLE. Six weeks ago. Paul – Mr. Rondine – is still threatening to press charges. Have me arrested.

SAM. It was an accident. He's got nothing on you –

CHELLE. I still live there.

I still live in that house.

I haven't been able to get away.

>   *(**SAM** stares at her.)*

That's why I called you.

I need your help.

>   *(A letter.)*

>   *(**MIRANDA** is alone, in a shaft of light, facing the audience.)*

>   *(Sound of waves crashing against the rocks.)*

MIRANDA. Today I saw the Mediterranean for the first time.

As I swam in its waters…I suddenly felt very far away from my own life.

MIRANDA. Far from the noise and madness of the accident, the search, the blame.

Far from all that has happened.

I told you I was planning to leave.
But not like this.

It was never meant to be like this.

Paul thinks I'm in Colorado with my sister.
No one – *no one but you* – knows where I really am.
I'm hoping, once again, you will keep my secret.

You were put in a terrible position.
We expected you to save our son.
And there was no way for you to do that.

I have time to think about this now.
Here where time moves more slowly.
Here on the waters of the Mediterranean.

7.

(Now.)

(SAM *and* **MITCH** *are at a bar, holding beers.)*

MITCH. *(With a laugh.)* She thinks you are a WHAT?!

SAM. Yeah – I know – it's crazy –

MITCH. And you just played along?

SAM. Like you told me to!

MITCH. And then I assume you ran like hell! Wow – you took one for the team there, Sammy!

(MITCH *clinks Sam's beer with his.)*

Tell me: what is it you really do for work?

SAM. Catering.

MITCH. Like you own a catering company?

SAM. Like I work for catering company. A couple of them. Picking up whatever shifts I can. Weddings. Parties. Bar Mitzvahs. I know that's not very exciting –

MITCH. Hey – it's cool.

SAM. – not like you – not like *espionage* –

MITCH. *Security*, Sam.

SAM. – but things just haven't – I wanted – I planned to go back to school. I wanted to study journalism – maybe try to –

MITCH. *Journalism?* Do they still teach that?

SAM. Investigative stuff.

MITCH. Yeah, well –

SAM. *(With an odd passion.)* Have you ever worked with *microfiche?*

MITCH. Have I *what?*

SAM. I interned at a paper that had all their old issues preserved on *microfiche.* Miniaturized pages – perfect little snapshots on film. And not digital – no software required – which means they'll be readable *forever.* What's more – and you will love this: *they are virtually impossible to destroy.*

MITCH. I believe times have changed, Sam.

SAM. Yeah, but it's a shame.

MITCH. Yeah, but now we are catering.

(Beat. They drink their beers.)

I bet you fold one hell of a napkin.

SAM. Yes, I do! But, hey, I'm curious: in your line of work –

MITCH. Whoa-whoa-whoa! You're not seeing this girl again, are you?

(Off **SAM**'s *look.)*

Oh, god, Sammy – you gotta move on from things! First the ex-girlfriend – then the *tiny fish* – and now this Chelle woman –

SAM. Hey –

MITCH. *(Continuous.)* – who is nothing but a neon sign flashing "Trouble." You've gotta stay the hell away from some deranged beauty who wants you to whack her husband!

SAM. He is not her husband! And of course I'm not gonna go through with it – I just thought –

MITCH. *You just thought WHAT?* What's your move now? Seems like she's been pretty upfront about what she wants from you –

SAM. – I know – but I was thinking you might –

MITCH. *(Continuous.)* – and even still – say you do it – say you somehow transform from Sammy the Caterer to Sammy the Assassin –

SAM. *I am not going to –*

MITCH. *(Continuous.)* – the truth of the matter is this:

If you want to hurt a guy, you don't kill him.

You *ruin him.*

His reputation.

His standing.

His power and stature in the world.

Who's the guy?

SAM. His name is Paul Rondine. He's a –

MITCH. *No way.*

SAM. You know him?

MITCH. Paul Rondine founded a company called *ClearHistory®*. The foremost data removal service in the world.

If you're a company, conglomerate, even a small nation-state – you bring him the data you want to make disappear, and he clears your history.

SAM. So I'd be trying to get dirt on the guy who is the master of getting rid of dirt.

MITCH. Exactly.

SAM. So what am I going to do? Chelle is trapped there, Mitch. She needs to get away.

MITCH. Then throw her in the trunk of your car in the middle of the night!

SAM. She's afraid he'll come after her. That he'll press charges –

MITCH. *There is something she's not telling you, Sam.* But you can't see that, because *you have fallen* –

SAM. No – that's not –

MITCH. *(Continuous.)* – fallen for this woman who let a little boy fall from a balcony –

SAM. It was not her fault!

MITCH. You don't know that!

> *(Before* **SAM** *can respond.)* No – listen to me: *you really do not know that.* All you *know* is that the wife is gone – and Chelle's got this rich guy all to herself. Nice house, nice car, sweet life.

> *(***SAM** *is staring hard at* **MITCH**.*)*

My advice is this: walk away. Walk away right now while you still can.

But if you don't – keep in mind:

You kill a guy...he's gone.

It's over and done.

But you *ruin* a guy...and he *suffers.*

He suffers and you get to watch.

Everyone gets to watch.

8.

(Then.)

*(**MIRANDA** and **PAUL** sit next to each other in plastic chairs. They are in the hallway of a police station.)*

(There is a long silence between them.)

PAUL. How long do they want us to wait?

MIRANDA. Patrick said they had forms for me to sign.

For us to sign.

(Beat.)

PAUL. Patrick?

MIRANDA. The sheriff.

PAUL. You know him as Patrick? This cop. This guy in charge of trying to find our son. Pretty bad at his job. Sitting in his office while our son is out there somewhere – in that water –

MIRANDA. The divers are out again. The helicopters. Coast Guard. They are doing everything they –

PAUL. Could you please *grieve*?

*(Off **MIRANDA**'s look.)*

I mean – jesus, Miranda – could you please just *fall apart a little bit?!* Sure – everyone is applauding you for how strong you're being in the face of all this – but really – did Alex not mean –

MIRANDA. *That boy means everything to me.*

You know that.

You've always known that.

(**PAUL** *looks away. Silence.*)

PAUL. We made threats to each other.

We put Alex in the middle of our fights.

And why? Why did we feel a need to do that?

Look at this...look at us now...look what we're left with...

You wanted to leave.

I know you did.

Please don't leave me.

(**A VOICE** *from offstage.*)

A VOICE. Mr. Rondine?

(**PAUL** *turns and looks offstage.*)

Could we see you in here, please?

(**PAUL** *looks at* **MIRANDA**. *Then he stands and leaves.*)

(**MIRANDA** *sits there, alone, for a moment. Then...*)

(**CHELLE** *arrives. She wears a scarf on her head, and a long coat.*)

CHELLE. Is there any more word?

(**MIRANDA** *does not look at* **CHELLE**.)

I haven't seen you.

I think they kept me away.

Kept us apart during the questioning.

God...they asked so many questions.

MIRANDA. Why was he out there? Why was Alexander playing on that balcony? *You knew that was off-limits.*

(**CHELLE** *is silent.*)

The sheriff told me you didn't see anything.

That you didn't see it happen.

CHELLE. No. By the time I –

(*Stops, beat.*)

When I got to the balcony...he had already fallen.

MIRANDA. What did Paul do?

(*Off* **CHELLE***'s look.*)

After it happened. When he heard you screaming.

CHELLE. He came running out of the house – he grabbed me – asked me what happened –

MIRANDA. Paul came running out of the house? Are you sure?

CHELLE. Yes – he was suddenly right behind me – I was looking down over the railing – and he grabbed me from behind – *he was shaking me* –

MIRANDA. But you didn't see him come out onto the balcony?

CHELLE. – no – I don't know – it was so fast – I was just –

MIRANDA. *Could he have been out there already?*

(*Before* **CHELLE** *can respond.*) Could Paul have been hiding on that balcony, too?

(**PAUL** *enters, slowly. He is holding a clear plastic bag which contains a few small items.*)

(**PAUL** *looks down at the plastic bag in his hands.*)

PAUL. *(Quietly.)* That's all.

That's everything.

His cap.

One shoe.

A little bit of a T-shirt.

Remember it?...that little yellow shirt we got him at the beach. It had those fish?...dolphins?...with the little bubbles coming out of their mouths...he loved that shirt...he slept in it...he never wanted to take it off...

(His voice trails away.)

(**PAUL** *carefully hands the plastic bag to* **MIRANDA**.*)*

(A long moment of stillness.)

(Then – after a look at **CHELLE** *–* **PAUL** *walks away and is gone.)*

(Neither of the women watch him go.)

MIRANDA. Go on with your life, Michelle.

You have any money?

CHELLE. What? – god – I'm not thinking about –

MIRANDA. If you need money, I'll give it to you.

Take it and get out.

(Before **CHELLE** *can respond.)*

You think I'm forgiving you.

I'm not.

CHELLE. I don't understand –

MIRANDA. Sure you do.

Get away from us.

(**MIRANDA** *stands and leaves, as –*)

9.

(Now.)

*(– **SAM** joins **CHELLE** at a casual pizza joint.)*

*(**CHELLE** continues to wear the scarf on her head. She has not taken off her coat.)*

CHELLE. You're late again.

SAM. Sorry.

CHELLE. I don't like it when people are late.

SAM. New place, huh? How's the pizza?

CHELLE. We're not going to eat.

SAM. Why not?

CHELLE. We're finished – you and me. It's over.

SAM. No – wait a minute –

CHELLE. Sitting here – waiting for you again – I realized: God – what a ridiculous idea! Having someone killed?! What kind of person *does something like that?!* Except *you*, maybe. And that's *awful*, Rick – you know that?! What you do for a living is *awful*. I can't believe I called you.

SAM. You're right – I agree with you –

CHELLE. Okay, then –

SAM. I don't think we should kill him.

I think it would be better to *ruin him.*

> *(Beat.)*

CHELLE. What did you say?

SAM. He's holding this threat over you, right? – that he can press charges for negligence. What if we found something you could *use against him?* Something from his past.

CHELLE. *(A hard laugh.)* From his *past?!* Do you know who this guy is?!

SAM. Yes, I do –

CHELLE. Do you know what his company *does?!*

SAM. – yes, of course – I've done my research –

> *(**CHELLE** suddenly puts her phone to her ear, as though on a call.)*

CHELLE. Take out your phone. Pretend to make a call.

SAM. What?

CHELLE. Just do it.

> *(**SAM** take out his phone. Holds it to his ear. He looks at her.)*

Keep looking forward.

SAM. But –

CHELLE. Don't look at me, Rick. *I mean it.*

> *(They sit there with their phones to their ears, staring front.)*

This is stupid, right? Acting like this.

SAM. Pretty stupid.

CHELLE. So do you get it? *These stupid things are my life now.* I have to pretend I'm not here meeting with you – because two of Paul's security guys are across the street with a camera.

SAM. *(Starting to turn.)* Really? – *where?*

CHELLE. Don't look. *Jesus, Rick.* I thought you knew how to do this.

>*(They sit there, phones to their ears – as they talk to one another.)*

SAM. Let me get you out of here.

CHELLE. Where will I go where Paul's "guys" won't find me?

SAM. To the police.

CHELLE. So they can question me again? – charge me with something?!

SAM. To report this – get a restraining order –

CHELLE. No way. I watched my mom go through that for years. Trying to keep us safe from my father. *What a joke.*

SAM. There must be someone you can stay with – a relative or a friend –

CHELLE. That's not an option –

SAM. Stay with me.

>*(Beat.)*

CHELLE. That's a terrible idea.

>*(**CHELLE** sets her phone down. She takes the scarf off her head.)*

You can hang up now.

They've left.

>*(**CHELLE** begins to fiddle nervously with a paper napkin on the table.)*

>*(**SAM** notices this.)*

SAM. There's something you're not telling me. Like why you're staying in that house.

Chelle...*please.*

(**SAM** *stares at her, waiting.*)

(**CHELLE** *stops fiddling with the paper napkin.*)

CHELLE. After the search was called off...and after the memorial service...I got my things together, and I started to leave the house.

10.

(Then.)

(**PAUL** *is at home. His tone – at first – is cold, impersonal.)*

(**CHELLE** *enters – moving toward a duffle-bag and small cardboard box.)*

PAUL. Is that the last of it?

CHELLE. Yes.

PAUL. I think we still owe you something.

(**PAUL** *takes some bills from his wallet.)*

CHELLE. Please don't do that. I don't want your money.

(**CHELLE** *gathers up her belongings.)*

PAUL. The memorial service was lovely.

Very hard, but...still.

I'm sure you understand why you were not invited.

Miranda was inconsolable.

She left the next morning.

She's gone to be with her sister in Colorado.

(Silence.)

And now...all this quiet.

(Silence.)

CHELLE. I still hear his voice. Just now...when I was upstairs. I could still hear the way he'd laugh when he ran through the halls.

PAUL. They say in everyone's life there is *one good death.* One necessary loss.

It is harder and harder for me to believe that.

Camus said the only true question is deciding whether or not life is worth living. Some nights now...when I stand on that balcony and look down at the water below...I wonder what my answer to that question will be...I wonder why I don't just let myself fall.

> (**PAUL** *holds out the money to* **CHELLE**.)

> (**CHELLE** *does not take it.*)

> (**PAUL** *sets the bills on a surface in the room. This surface also contains an official-looking manila envelope.*)

Do you still read Camus?

CHELLE. No.

PAUL. Did you ever?

> (*Off* **CHELLE**'*s look.*)

I called your references. They were fake. All lies. It seems you're nothing but a desperate young woman on the run. And *not even that young* as it turns out.

I've done what I can. Given your name to a few people.

CHELLE. I didn't ask you to do that –

PAUL. The case is in the hands of a new person now. A homicide detective –

CHELLE. *Homicide?*

PAUL. – and he'll no doubt have some questions for you.

CHELLE. Wait – no –

PAUL. There's the charge of criminal negligence, of course. But there's also the suspicion of foul play. That could bring a charge of manslaughter.

>   (**CHELLE** *prepares to leave –*)

CHELLE. Goodbye, Mr. Rondine –

PAUL. Don't forget your money. It's there, on the top of the summons you received.

>   (*This stops* **CHELLE**.)

You should open it. The date of the hearing will be in there. If you miss it, they can find you in contempt.

>   (**CHELLE** *takes the summons. She starts out of the room –*)

And you should leave the jewelry with me.

CHELLE. What jewelry?

PAUL. Miranda thought she'd misplaced those necklaces and bracelets. Maybe lent them to a friend. But I found them yesterday.

They were in a little plastic bucket, covered over with trinkets, in the very bottom of Alex's toy box.

Something that was never disturbed. You of all people would have known that.

CHELLE. None of that has anything to –

PAUL. *– Anything to do with a boy falling from a balcony?* No. Maybe not. But when the new detective takes a closer look at the person who was in charge of Alex's safety – I think he'll see that you *just don't add up*, Michelle. Or whatever your real name is.

>   (**CHELLE** *reaches into her bag. She removes a scarf in which some items are bundled.*)

(This is the same scarf she was wearing in Scene 9.)

Open it, please.

*(**CHELLE** opens the scarf...revealing several pieces of expensive jewelry.)*

They were all gifts. One for each of our anniversaries. You should have seen her face...*the way it just lit up...*

Did you ever wear them? Even one of the necklaces?

CHELLE. No.

PAUL. You should. They would look good on you.

*(**PAUL** is staring at **CHELLE**...trying to read her reaction.)*

What? What did I say?

CHELLE. *(Challenging him.)* And the dresses...those blue dresses in Miranda's closet. Would they look good on me, too?

PAUL. They would, in fact.

(An odd standoff.)

CHELLE. You are out of line.

PAUL. Yes – I'm sure I am –

CHELLE. You are *way* out of line.

PAUL. – I'm sorry –

CHELLE. *(Strong.)* Whatever you think you *see* when you look at me, it's –

PAUL. Should I tell you?

I can tell you what I see.

I see someone who spent their childhood in fear.

PAUL. Constantly on the run. Someone who hasn't felt safe in a long time.

CHELLE. How do you know those things about me?

PAUL. How do I know anything? I watch. I inquire.

That older man was outside the gates again. He was asking about you. Seems determined to find you. I had him sent away. We've re-coded the alarm system, as a precaution.

His name is Charles Raymond Latimer.

Uses a variety of aliases.

Divorced.

Widowed.

One grown daughter.

Your father has quite the police record.

And like you: he's still on the run.

>   (**CHELLE** *is staring at* **PAUL.**)

I never mentioned the jewelry to the police. And I've worked things out with the detective, for now – kept him from pressing charges.

CHELLE. *I didn't ask you to do any of that!*

PAUL. You may not care for me, Chelle.

But you have come to need me, haven't you?

>   (**PAUL** *lifts the bills and places them inside* **CHELLE**'s *cardboard box – along with the jewelry.*)

Star – nine – seven – five – forty-two – eleven.

That's the new code.

CHELLE. Why are you telling me that?

PAUL. Stay here.

It's a big house.

You can see me, or not.

Whatever you prefer.

Stay as long as you want.

Leave when you want to leave.

(**PAUL** *lifts the manilla envelope.*)

Shall I make this [that] summons go away?

CHELLE. Why would you do that?

I thought you wanted to punish me.

PAUL. I thought so, too.

11.

(Now. Continuous from Scene 10.)

*(**CHELLE** turns back to **SAM** at the pizza joint.)*

SAM. And you stayed.

CHELLE. I thought I could find something to use against him. There was a storage room off the garage. Inside I found a suitcase.

This suitcase was packed for a long trip of some kind. *And all the clothes belonged to Alexander.*

There was a folder with Alexander's birth certificate and health records. And the strangest thing: there was a list of new names and social security numbers – like he was going to give Alex a new identity.

SAM. He was planning to kidnap his son.

CHELLE. What else could it be?

SAM. But he didn't get the chance. Before he could do it, the boy fell.

CHELLE. *Or did he?* I keep thinking about what Miranda asked me – if maybe Paul was *hiding out there* the day it happened.

SAM. Hiding out there to do what?

CHELLE. I don't know. He would never hurt his son. But it was *Paul's idea* to let Alex play out on the balcony that day. I never told Miranda that.

SAM. What about the security cameras?

CHELLE. The police checked. The day it happened, the cameras were not working.

SAM. *That one day?!* The one day it mattered?!

CHELLE. What if he staged it somehow? The accident. The fall.

SAM. But why would he need to do that?! He's rich – powerful –

CHELLE. Yes, but –

SAM. *(Continuous.)* – if he wanted custody of his son, he'd just pull some strings – make it happen.

CHELLE. Unless she has something on him.

Something that could ruin him.

> *(This lands with* **SAM**.*)*

I'm getting letters from her.

> *(Off* **SAM**'s *look.)*

She's not in Colorado. She went to France. Told no one.

SAM. And she's writing to you at the house?

CHELLE. Yes – Paul doesn't know. The letters just show up in my bag.

SAM. And you don't know who puts them there?

CHELLE. No.

> *(Silence, as* **CHELLE** *turns and looks away.)*

SAM. Is Paul right? Is your father looking for you?

> *(***CHELLE** *turns back to* **SAM**.*)*

CHELLE. When do I get to learn things about you?

SAM. Like what?

CHELLE. Like how'd you get into this line of work?

SAM. Unexpectedly.

> *(***SAM** *leans in to her.)*

SAM. I can't help you if you don't tell me things.

> (**CHELLE** *says nothing. Once again, she begins to fiddle with the paper napkin on the table.*)

Have you heard of "normalcy bias"?

CHELLE. Oh, c'mon, Rick –

SAM. Normalcy Bias is what makes us constantly *underestimate our own peril*. We do that because we believe somehow – in some way – things will always *return to Normal.*

CHELLE. – okay, well –

SAM. They won't. They *don't*.

CHELLE. *(Dark, strong.)* – hey – you know what? "Normalcy" is a *luxury I've just never had*. My mom and I would have *killed* for a little normalcy – but there was no chance of that with my father around. We ran away from him when I was nine. New names. New schools. Always on the move.

When I was fifteen, my mom dropped me off at a shelter in Cincinnati and headed south: *"Lay low, Shelly. Lay low. Keep moving. And, whatever you do: never let your father find you."*

On the day when Alexander went out to hide on that balcony...the phone rang.

I listened for only a few seconds.

But I know it was my father.

> (**CHELLE** *sets the napkin aside.*)

So...yes...I am staying with Paul in that house.

Star – nine – seven – five – forty-two – eleven.

And the hell of it is: for the first time in my life I feel safe. *God – how quickly we can accommodate ourselves to the things we thought we'd hate.*

(**SAM** *is looking into* **CHELLE***'s eyes.*)

You should see your face.

The way you look at me...

Why do you look at me like that?

SAM. I can't help it.

(*Beat.*)

CHELLE. I'm sorry it happened like this.

The way we met.

SAM. I think our paths would have crossed.

One way or another.

CHELLE. Oh, god. You're one of those people, aren't you?
The kind who just *expect good things to happen.*

SAM. I don't know – maybe.

CHELLE. I'm not.

I'm not one of those people.

I'm glad to know you, Rick.

But the thing is – meeting this way – we'll have to lie.

We'll have to deny that we ever met.

SAM. I need to tell you the truth.

(**CHELLE** *is waiting.*)

CHELLE. Okay...

SAM. I haven't done this.

I mean...

(**CHELLE** *waits.*)

SAM. ...as much as I let on.

(**CHELLE** *leans in to him.*)

CHELLE. And I haven't done this at all.

(*A letter.*)

(**MIRANDA** *stands, alone, as before.*)

(*Sound of waves crashing against the rocks.*)

MIRANDA. Paul would hate that I'm writing you letters.

He hates paper.

He doesn't trust it.

In our business, Paul says, *paper is the hardest thing to wipe clean.*

I used to think that names mattered.
Turns out: they don't.

I have a new name here. I use this name in the mornings. Then I use another name in the afternoons, at the beach. Still another name at night, in the cafes.

But our names can't hide who we are.

No matter what I am called...I know in my heart that I'm still a woman who chose a man named Paul Rondine.

(**PAUL'S VOICE** – *from the next scene* – *is heard...*)

PAUL'S VOICE. Miranda, is that you?

MIRANDA. I tried to run from my life – just like you.

PAUL'S VOICE. I thought you were going out.

MIRANDA. But Paul will always find me. Just like he will always find you.

PAUL'S VOICE. Are you back already?

12.

(Then.)

*(**PAUL** is at home, working at his laptop.)*

*(**MIRANDA** enters with her purse over her shoulder, holding her car keys.)*

MIRANDA. Can I use your phone? I must have left mine at the gym.

PAUL. Sure – everything okay?

MIRANDA. My car won't start. Do you think it's the battery inside the little fob-thing?

PAUL. Could be. Do you have another key?

MIRANDA. Maybe I can borrow your car and drive down to the gym.

PAUL. Do you want Chelle to take you?

MIRANDA. She's playing with Alexander. I don't want to disturb them.

*(**PAUL** takes out his own phone.)*

PAUL. Let me try calling your phone. Before you waste a trip down there.

MIRANDA. You don't have to do that –

PAUL. Or I could drop you somewhere. Where were you going?

MIRANDA. Nowhere – some errands –

PAUL. Not down the coast to see your friend?

The nice sheriff. The big man in that little town. You volunteered at that fund raiser for them –

MIRANDA. For the *library* down there –

PAUL. – and I know he was very grateful. He sent you a note of thanks.

MIRANDA. No, he didn't.

PAUL. Sure he did. I can show it to you.

MIRANDA. What the hell, Paul? *You're going through my mail?*

PAUL. He's married, you know. His wife's a lawyer. They have two kids.

MIRANDA. How do you know that?

PAUL. How do I know *anything*, Miranda? I *watch*. I *learn*. I *pay attention*.

Maybe he'll answer if I call your phone. Is that what you're afraid of? That I'll find out about the two of you.

MIRANDA. There's nothing to find out!

PAUL. You're right. He probably wouldn't answer. Since your phone is here.

> (**PAUL** *removes Miranda's phone from his pocket.*)

MIRANDA. *You're sick*. You know that?

PAUL. I've made a nice life for you, Miranda. But you are ruining it –

MIRANDA. I'm doing no such thing!

PAUL. *(Continuous.)* – ruining it with all the attention you are giving these men – this sheriff – the guys who work for me –

MIRANDA. You're delusional! – none of that is –

PAUL. *(Continuous.)* – but that is not how this is going to work. Yes – I've taken your phone. And I've disabled your car. You are not to –

MIRANDA. I'll climb the fence, you fucker! I'll get away –
*and I'll take Alexander – and you will never see either
of us again.*

That hurts, right?

The thought of losing your son.

I bet that just *kills you.*

> (*And now, unseen by* **MIRANDA** *and* **PAUL**,
> **CHELLE** *appears. She is on her way through
> the room, carrying something for Alex.*)

> (*Hearing their conversation,* **CHELLE** *stops.
> Listens.*)

This paranoia – these *resentments* – where did all this
come from? You resent me for, what? – *sharing a life
with you? – sharing a house? – a company*?

You know, I kept that cocktail napkin.

The one from the bar at the Fairmont Hotel.

The one with *my writing on it.*

The one with the algorithm *I invented.*

I put it in my keepsake box as a souvenir.

But now it is gone.

And I'm not surprised.

You've been clearing our history, haven't you? – a little
bit at a time – until nowadays most people assume our
company was created entirely by you: *the great Paul
Rondine.*

> (*Now:* **CHELLE** *continues through the room,
> quietly.* **MIRANDA** *and* **PAUL** *have not seen
> her.*)

MIRANDA. You can have that history, Paul – I don't want it anymore. What I want to know is this:

Where did that man go?

The man I first met. The man with enough guts to make me his wife, his partner.

I look around now...at everything we have...everything we've made...and I think:

I am in the wrong life.

> (*Silence.*)

I need to leave. And I need to take Alexander with me.

PAUL. That won't happen, Miranda.

MIRANDA. It *is* happening – I've been in touch with a lawyer –

PAUL. You are going to need something *much stronger than a lawyer* to take my son away from me. You are going to need *a much better plan than that.*

> (**MIRANDA** *is staring at him.*)

Go tell them, Miranda. Go tell your story to the world!

It won't matter.

Because the story they *want* – and the story they are *always going to believe* – is that I met a smart woman, top of her class at Stanford, but now she was staring at middle-age with no idea how to make her life match her ambition. Then, one day in the bar of a San Francisco hotel, she hit on a truly remarkable idea. But it fell to *me* to push it forward. Because this woman *did not know how to make things happen.*

She still doesn't.

You still don't.

13.

(Now.)

*(**MITCH** and **SAM** are at Sam's apartment. Mitch's laptop is open.)*

MITCH. What about Rondine's wife? Where was she when the boy fell?

SAM. At the DMV – getting her license renewed.

MITCH. You have proof of that.

SAM. I went there – checked it out.

MITCH. And the DMV just *gave you that information?*

SAM. I know a guy. I cater with a guy who works at the DMV.

MITCH. *(Impressed.)* Whoa! – Sammy the Napkin Folder!

(Re: his laptop.)

Let me show you what I found on the surveillance tape.

SAM. I thought the cameras on the balcony were not working that day.

MITCH. The cameras were working fine. But someone got hold of the footage. *And they wiped it clean.*

(Ironically.)

Now, who would do that, I wonder?! Lucky for us, the original file was encrypted and hadn't been touched. I got it from the company overseas that runs the server.

SAM. *How did you do that?*

MITCH. Just like you, Sammy: I know a guy.

Check this out.

(On the laptop screen.)

MITCH. There's the little boy alone on the balcony. Running around – smiling – looking for a place to hide. And then – watch – he gets startled by something. He turns. He's looking another direction. Not toward the house.

SAM. Someone must be talking to him.

MITCH. But we never see who it is. And...here...after a few seconds, he takes off his cap – throws it off the balcony – and then he walks out of the frame.

SAM. Toward the voice, the person –

MITCH. Yep.

SAM. – toward the stairs leading down, off the side of the balcony.

MITCH. Stairs which – again, on this one day – *do not show up on the security feed.*

SAM. It means the boy's not dead.

MITCH. *(Smiles.)* It looks that way, Sammy.

(**MITCH** *is packing up his laptop.*)

SAM. This is amazing! Once we give this to the police, they can –

MITCH. *We have committed crimes getting this video –*

SAM. Yeah, but when they see –

MITCH. *(Continuous.)* – but here's what you can do: you can tell Chelle it was not her fault – that Rondine's *got nothing on her –*

SAM. But if we have the –

MITCH. *(Continuous.)* – and there's one more thing that will seal the deal: *we have to get that suitcase she found.* It's proof that Rondine wanted to abduct his kid. We don't want Chelle to do something stupid with that suitcase.

SAM. She won't do that.

MITCH. Based on what? *How very well you know her?!* Did it ever dawn on you that maybe *you're* the one who's being *played?* She doesn't care about you, Sam! She thinks she's hanging out with some guy named "Rick" – sitting with him at the park – enjoying the pleasure of his company at all these coffee houses and pizza joints–

SAM. Wait – how do you know that? –

MITCH. *(Continuous.)* – and then every night she is going home to Paul Rondine!

SAM. Mitch – *answer me!* –

    *(**MITCH** is gone.)*

14.

(Then.)

*(**MIRANDA** at home. She is removing yellow daffodils from their vase, and tossing them in a waste basket.)*

*(**CHELLE** is walking through the room. She carries Alexander's black Mickey Mouse cap.)*

MIRANDA. Any luck with the napping today?

CHELLE. *(With a smile.)* Alexander the Great is out like a light. It took awhile. He had something he was trying to remember. But he didn't know what to call that feeling. It made me think there must be a moment when we first realize that we can *forget things.* But he didn't have a word for it, so he just kept saying: *"There was a thing...there was a thing..."*

MIRANDA. You're very good with him.

CHELLE. *(The flowers.)* You're throwing those out? They still look lovely.

MIRANDA. They've served their purpose.

*(**MIRANDA** continues her work.)*

CHELLE. Always daffodils.

Always yellow.

It's a great story.

You and Paul at the hotel bar.

The idea scribbled on the back of a cocktail napkin.

It was an algorithm or something?

MIRANDA. Yes.

CHELLE. And it was you.

It was your writing.

> (**MIRANDA** *turns to her.*)

You created the company.

> *(Beat.)*

MIRANDA. Paul will want you to stay here when I'm gone.

CHELLE. Gone where?

MIRANDA. Be smart, Chelle: a man like Paul is used to having exactly what he wants. And one of those things is to *never be left alone.*

CHELLE. But –

MIRANDA. You need to be ready for that. No matter what else happens.

> (**PAUL** *enters, dressed casually. He is carrying some children's picture books.*)

PAUL. There you are. I was looking for Alex –

MIRANDA. He's napping. And I was just telling Chelle that I'll be gone most of the day tomorrow. I need to go to the DMV. Get my license renewed. Oh, joy. I'll be gone all afternoon.

PAUL.	**CHELLE.**
All right.	It's fine. I'll be here.

MIRANDA. *(To* **CHELLE.***)* Alexander will want to play Hide-N-Seek with you, of course. Anywhere *except* on the far balcony. That balcony is still off-limits. Understood?

CHELLE. Yes. Of course.

> *(Lightly.)*

He'll just hide in the coat closet, anyway.

MIRANDA. Yes – that's true.

>   (*To* **PAUL**.)

See you in a bit.

>   (**MIRANDA** *leaves.*)

CHELLE. Alex just went down. But if you want me to –

PAUL. No. It's fine. Let him sleep.

And, listen…tomorrow – if he wants to play out on that balcony: *let him do it*. It's perfectly safe – it's all to code –

CHELLE. Yes, but –

PAUL. – and why should his mother's fears become his fears? You'll be with him. He'll be fine.

We don't need to tell Miranda.

All right?

>   (*Beat.*)

CHELLE. Sure.

>   (**CHELLE** *starts to leave –*)

PAUL. Listen – there seems to be someone looking for you. Older man. Dark clothes. My security team spotted him – just outside the gate – checking out the property. He was asking for you by the name of "Shelly".

>   (**CHELLE** *stops, but says nothing.*)

Someone you know?

CHELLE. No.

>   (*Beat.*)

PAUL. It's odd. I've watched for years as people had their own past weaponized against them – and for what reason? Why should our history hold such needless power over us?

(*Approaching* **CHELLE**.)

If you ever want to make a new start – for your own safety...just let me know.

CHELLE. (*A hard stare.*) Thank you.

(**CHELLE** *goes and* –)

15.

(Now.)

*(– **CHELLE** joins **SAM** at an upscale hip bistro
– wine glasses, cloth napkins, trendy menus.)*

SAM. You're late.

CHELLE. Yes, I know I'm late –

SAM. I was afraid something had happened.

CHELLE. Something did happen. My car wouldn't start.

SAM. Why?

CHELLE. No idea. I pressed the little fob thing – *nothing*. So I walked out the gate and down the drive. Called for a ride down here. Paul's guys don't know about this place.

SAM. You're sure?

CHELLE. I'm never sure.

> *(As before, **CHELLE** lifts one of the napkins and begins to fold it.)*

SAM. This place is very hip.

Or I am very not hip

> *(**CHELLE** is still folding.)*

(The napkin.) Why do you do that?

CHELLE. Just nervous energy. And it's much better when they are cloth.

> *(As she folds.)*

There are people who are really good at this, you know. They can fold, like, a rose. Or a pocket. Or a crown.

SAM. I didn't know that.

CHELLE. What do you think of the name "Riley"? "Riley Marie Carpenter." Paul says he can build me a new history – passport, birth certificate, new Social – with whatever name I choose.

SAM. I hope you told him all of that is bullshit –

CHELLE. What's bullshit is spending my whole life on the run!

(**SAM** *grabs the napkin from her –*)

SAM. *Listen to me –*

CHELLE. – and – hey – you know what else?

Last night I got a call from Rick.

Rick said he'd bumped into Pablo and Skip at the gym and they asked about me. Rick said: "Oh, yeah, right, I never got back to her."

(*She sets a napkin in front of* **SAM.**)

Here. Make me a little Rose.

(*Angered.*)

I trusted you. I told you everything –

SAM. Hey – you're the one who wouldn't tell me things –

CHELLE. *(Continuous.)* – and you've been – what? – just playing some kind of game?! Who does something like that?!

SAM. *(Continuous.)* – no – no – don't put that on me – you're the one who's been playing GAMES here!

CHELLE. Well – thank you, *SAM!* Thank you for that amazing insight – *Mister SAM ARNETT-*

SAM. Wait –

CHELLE. *(Continuous.) – itinerant caterer – Journalism School dropout.*

SAM. Yes – I am all those things! – *I am all those things at once* – I'm an idiot who saw you sitting at a coffee shop – and now I know that Mitch was right –

CHELLE. *Who the hell is Mitch?*

SAM. *(Continuous.)* – that I should have walked away when I had the chance. Rondine isn't trying to protect you! – he's determined to keep you close to him so he can –

CHELLE. So he can *what? Talk* with me? *Spend time* with me? Give me *"the pleasure of his company?"* How is that any different than *you?*

SAM. It's different.

CHELLE. *How?*

(*Beat.*)

SAM. It's just *very different.*

I know these guys, Chelle. I've studied them. That jewelry you took from his wife – that's going to become *your* jewelry. Those blue dresses are going to become *your* blue dresses. And somewhere in the room is going to be a vase of yellow flowers. It's called –

SAM.	**CHELLE.**
(Continued.) – "repetition compulsion" – but even still – the thing is:	Yes – we've all seen *Vertigo*, Sam –

SAM. *(Continued.) We know that he blackmailed you into staying with him.*

Alexander did not fall from that balcony.

(*Before* **CHELLE** *can respond.*)

SAM. I don't know where he is – I don't know if he's still alive – but I've seen the real video of that day, the one Paul did not wipe clean – and that boy *did not fall.*

It was not your fault.

Paul has been using it to keep you in that house.

And Charles Raymond Latimer – your Dad – who you've been running from:

Shot and killed three years ago, outside a bar in Baton Rouge.

Victim of an extortion plot.

Dead at age fifty-six.

Next of kin unknown.

> *(Beat.)*

CHELLE. *(Quietly.)* Three years ago?

SAM. It's all been a lie to make you think you were in danger.

> **(CHELLE** *looks away.)*

And I lied to you, too.

I'm sorry.

I know I won't see you again.

> *(Off* **CHELLE**'s *look.)*

I just...I *got caught up in it.*

And in you.

> **(SAM** *stands, preparing to leave.)*

You can leave that house now.

CHELLE. *(Quietly.)* Yes.

SAM. He's got nothing on you.

CHELLE. Right.

> (**SAM** *starts off, and is almost gone when* **CHELLE** *says:*)

But I still want to ruin him.

> (*An odd moment of silence. Then...***SAM** *sits back down at the table.*)

SAM. Okay.

> (**SAM** *leans in to her.*)

What does Miranda know that we don't?

CHELLE. Well, she started the company – not him. The algorithm – the famous cocktail napkin – that was all her.

SAM. So, he was telling the truth: his life *literally started* when he met Miranda.

What about *his life before that?*

CHELLE. She doesn't know. No one does.

SAM. They met at the Fairmont, right?

CHELLE. Yes – but it was ten years ago –

SAM. Those historic hotels keep an archive, sometimes. The old fashioned "guest book." Long-standing practice. If we can narrow down the date they stayed there – if you can get Paul to tell you the *month* even –

CHELLE. We know there were daffodils. Has to be spring. And Miranda said they got married three weeks later. So, if we knew their anniversary –

SAM. – right – then we could back-date it.

CHELLE. She was in room two oh five. His room was the numerical opposite.

SAM. Okay – good –

CHELLE. But even if you get the date –

SAM. – I lived out there – catered events at those hotels. It's a long shot, I know – Mitch would say *"forget about it, Sammy – that info has vanished!"* – but still –

CHELLE. Who is Mitch?

SAM. He put me up to this.

CHELLE. Why would he do that?

SAM. He was trying to help at first, I thought –

CHELLE. Wait – you involved him in this?

SAM. *(Continuous.)* – but now I think he's started to follow us – to watch us when we meet –

CHELLE. Oh my god, Sam –

SAM. *(Continuous.)* – and the thing is: *he keeps asking about that suitcase you found* – I don't know why –

CHELLE. Because you told him about it.

(**SAM** *says nothing.*)

You told him about the suitcase, right?

SAM. *(Realizes.)* No. I don't think I did.

CHELLE. He'd only know that if he worked for Paul.

16.

(Now.)

*(**PAUL** and **MITCH** stand together at home. **PAUL** is dressed nicely.)*

*(**PAUL** and **MITCH** are watching **CHELLE** – as she arrives with a large bundle of cut flowers, wrapped in paper. During what follows, **CHELLE** will unwrap yellow daffodils and place them in a vase.)*

*(**CHELLE** is not aware she is being watched. The image is similar to Scene 1.)*

PAUL. Have you ever spoken? Ever introduced yourself?

MITCH. To who?

PAUL. To Chelle. To this woman you are staring at.

MITCH. I wasn't staring. I was just –

(Stops.)

(Beat.)

PAUL. Are we still monitoring her car?

MITCH. Yes.

PAUL. Then how was she able to leave?

MITCH. She walked off the property. Called for a ride.

PAUL. She has a second phone?

MITCH. Apparently.

PAUL. And the sightings of her father?

MITCH. Ongoing. I've put together a few more surveillance photos.

PAUL. Good. Thank you, Mitch.

>   (**MITCH** *goes, walking right past –)*

>   (**CHELLE**, *who brings the vase into the room.)*

(Warmly.) There you are. I wondered where you'd gone. Your car was still in the garage.

CHELLE. It wouldn't start.

PAUL. That's odd.

CHELLE. Doesn't matter. I won't need it.

>   *(The flowers.)*

I passed the farmer's market and saw these. They made me think of Miranda. Have you heard from her? She's not in Colorado, you know. I think she's overseas.

PAUL. I doubt that.

CHELLE. It's strange you don't know where she is. After the way you tracked her every move.

PAUL. Miranda was always free to leave. Just like you are.

CHELLE. I'll be gone tomorrow.

PAUL. *(Bemused.)* Really? How will that work exactly? With your father still waiting to track you down.

CHELLE. I'll take my chances.

PAUL. I left you a list of possible names. Trust me: your old life will be the ruin of you – but once you choose a new one, you will never have to look back. You can make a new start.

CHELLE. Where?

Here?

How would that work exactly?

>   *(Silence. Standoff.)*

CHELLE. Miranda told me you have an anniversary coming up. Next month, I think.

PAUL. I'm not thinking about that, anymore.

CHELLE. I've been getting letters from her.

PAUL. That's impossible.

I would have known if you got a letter.

CHELLE. She mentioned your anniversary. Said maybe she'd be home by that date. I thought you'd want to know. Late-April, right? The twenty-fifth or sixth?

PAUL. *(Irritated.)* No – it's neither of those – and if she was coming home, I would have known.

CHELLE. Like you knew about the letters.

(**PAUL** *gives her a hard stare.*)

Did you want Alex all to yourself?

(*Off* **PAUL***'s look.*)

That was Miranda's fear. That you were going to take him away.

PAUL. That's ridiculous. I wanted him here. Wanted the three of us to be together.

CHELLE. Then what was the suitcase for?

Filled with Alex's clothes.

His paperwork.

Isn't that why you wanted him to play on the balcony? So you could steal him away from Miranda – give him a new identity –

PAUL. *What on earth are you saying –*

CHELLE. Alex is alive, isn't he?

Maybe I should give your name to some people.

Maybe I should tell the Sheriff.

Maybe he already knows.

(**CHELLE** *turns and goes, as –*)

17.

(Then.)

*(– **PAUL** joins **MIRANDA** at home.)*

*(**MIRANDA** hands **PAUL** a lovely necklace. She turns, allowing him to affix the necklace. They are dressed for an evening out. The mood is light and romantic.)*

PAUL. Chelle will be down in a few minutes.

MIRANDA. You were right after all.

PAUL. Hmm?

MIRANDA. Your idea to hire an *au pair*. It was a good one.

*(**MIRANDA** is looking in an [unseen] mirror, admiring her necklace.)*

Look at that. It's perfect.

I know I don't wear this jewelry as often as you'd like.

But, tonight I thought –

(She stops.)

Tonight is different.

*(**MIRANDA** touches **PAUL**'s face.)*

PAUL. Somewhere special then?

MIRANDA. Sure. You pick.

Can you get my shawl? It's in the hall closet.

*(**PAUL** goes.)*

MIRANDA. *(To* PAUL, *offstage.)* I'm hoping to get to the DMV by two or two-thirty tomorrow. It's always endless at the DMV. I'll bring a book. Then I think I might do a little shopping. I'll likely be gone all day. I know you need to work at home, but Chelle will be here.

> (PAUL *re-enters with a shawl, which he drapes over* MIRANDA'*s shoulders.)*

PAUL. Speaking of Chelle: Alex just raced up and jumped into her arms. Then he ran off to get his Mickey Mouse cap.

MIRANDA. Tell her we won't be late. And be sure to kiss your son goodnight.

PAUL. *(Finds this odd.)* I always do...

MIRANDA. He'll be asleep when we get home.

PAUL. Yes, I know...

MIRANDA. I'm just saying. These years go by so fast. And Alex will always love his Daddy.

> (MIRANDA *kisses him, tenderly, on the cheek. Then she leaves.)*
>
> *(A letter.)*
>
> (CHELLE *stands, alone. She wears a long coat.* CHELLE *holds a letter in her hands.)*
>
> *(The image is similar to the previous letters.)*
>
> *(Sound of waves crashing against the rocks.)*

CHELLE. *(Reading.)* "Dear Chelle,

If you are reading this, that means you are still in my house. I can only guess about your reasons for staying. But you should know:

A terrible thing has happened.

CHELLE. But it was not what you thought.

It was not what anyone thought.

I used to believe that the way to "start over" was to turn your back on the life you had.

But now I know it's the opposite of that.

You can never start over until you stare down your past."

(**MIRANDA'S VOICE** *is heard, from the darkness –*)

MIRANDA'S VOICE. It is a beautiful view.

18.

(Now.)

(– And now **MIRANDA** *is standing behind* **CHELLE** *on the balcony.* **MIRANDA** *is also wearing a long coat. She carries no purse or bag.)*

*(***CHELLE*** *turns to her, startled.)*

MIRANDA. I've tried to block it from my mind – but I can't.

CHELLE. When did you get back?

MIRANDA. Just last night. And you haven't left. No matter how much I warned you.

CHELLE. I'm leaving now.

MIRANDA. I see.

CHELLE. *I was blamed for what happened.* Paul has been threatening to press charges – have me arrested me for the death of your son –

MIRANDA. Yes, I know.

CHELLE. – NO – I don't think you do. You don't know that your son is alive, Miranda. That Paul took him – abducted him, somehow – had the video wiped clean – and then tried to make it look like my fault.

MIRANDA. Chelle – no –

CHELLE. And you were right: Paul must have been hiding out here on the balcony that day. I found a suitcase he had hidden away – packed with Alexander's clothes and paperwork –

MIRANDA. Paul didn't pack that suitcase.

I did.

CHELLE. *What?*

(**MITCH** *appears on the balcony.*)

MIRANDA. Good evening, Mitch.

CHELLE. *Mitch?* Oh my god. Leave us alone –

MIRANDA. It's fine.

CHELLE. – go back to your cave, or wherever Paul keeps you guys.

MIRANDA. Mitch is welcome to stay. He made sure you got my letters from France.

(**CHELLE** *looks again at* **MITCH**.)

MITCH. *(To* **MIRANDA**.*)* The cameras are turned off. Paul will be out in a minute.

MIRANDA. Thank you, Mitch

(To **CHELLE**.*)*

Most of the day went as planned.

I sent my sister to the DMV to check in under my name.

I knew Paul had a two p.m. call that he'd take in his office at the far end of the house. And I knew you would be here – playing Hide-N-Seek with Alexander.

I was waiting just outside the front door. I knew my son would hide in the closet, right by the door, and I would take him away.

But on that day – for some reason – he came out on this balcony instead.

I ran back here. I had Mitch call your phone to keep you occupied for another minute.

Alexander didn't want to stop playing. He got mad. As we were leaving, he threw his Mickey Mouse cap off the balcony. We left and met my sister at the airport.

MIRANDA. Paul would try to find us, of course – but I planned to clear our histories before he did. I knew a little something about that.

As our flight to France was boarding...I remembered the suitcase.

In my haste, I had left it behind.

And something else had happened.

CHELLE. What?

MIRANDA. You.

You had come out on that balcony.

And you had told Paul that his son had fallen.

CHELLE. Yes – because –

MIRANDA. Paul saw the cap down by the water.

And he believed you.

They all believed you.

The house was overrun with Police, EMTs, Search and Rescue units – they were all looking for my son, who I knew was at the airport, about to fly to France.

My sister and my son flew away. And I came back to a house I thought I'd never see again.

CHELLE. But the video? The clothes they found?

MIRANDA. I had Mitch alter the video.

And I had Alexander's clothes in my bag.

I gave them to the Sheriff.

He planted them down by the water.

I was asked to grieve.

MIRANDA. And I grieved.

I put together a memorial service.

I knew that if I told the truth…I'd surely lose my son to Paul.

CHELLE. So you played along.

MIRANDA. Yes. I had to.

CHELLE. *(Direct.)* You chose to.

And you put me in the middle of it.

MIRANDA. *(Nods, quietly.)* I'm sorry.

(*Tense beat. Standoff.*)

CHELLE. Is this where you swear me to secrecy?

MIRANDA. No more secrets. I came back to tell Paul what I've done.

CHELLE. But *why?* – you got away with it –

MIRANDA. I thought I could live with it.

Make a new start – just me and my son.

But I can't do it.

Not like this.

(**CHELLE** *stares at her.*)

CHELLE. And Alex? How is he?

MIRANDA. He's good.

CHELLE. Is he with you?

MIRANDA. No. But he's safe.

(**PAUL** *appears on the balcony –*)

PAUL'S VOICE. Miranda?! What is this? What are you doing?!

MIRANDA. I was just saying goodbye to Chelle.

She's leaving, you know.

PAUL. Where've you been all these weeks? No one could find you –

MIRANDA. I've been seeing all the things you told me about.

The blue of that water.

The heat of that sun.

But even on the other side of the world...I kept thinking about us.

How we treated each other.

It is much too late for us...but it should not have been too late for our son.

He deserved better.

I see that now.

PAUL. But here we are, Miranda.

It's not going to end differently.

MIRANDA. *It did.* It can.

(*Beat.*)

PAUL. *What are you saying?!*

(*Before* **MIRANDA** *can respond –*)

(**SAM** *appears. He wears a dark coat.*)

SAM. (*Buoyantly.*) Hey – wow – would you look at this place?!

CHELLE.   **MITCH.**
Oh my god!   What the hell?!

(**SAM** *turns to* **MITCH.**)

SAM. Hey, Mitch. How's it going?

CHELLE. *(To* **SAM.**) *What are you DOING here?*

SAM. *(Upbeat, to* **PAUL** *and* **MIRANDA.**) Nice house. Great view.

MIRANDA. *Who is this?!*

SAM. *(To the* **OTHERS.**) You can call me Rick.

PAUL. How'd you get in here?!

SAM. Star – nine – seven – five – forty-two – eleven. *Never forget the code* – right, Mitch?

   (*To* **PAUL**, *"RATS-luff".*)

So – how's your night going, *Mr. Ratzlaff?*

PAUL. What did you call me?

SAM. *Mr. Arnold Ratzlaff.* I know that was just one of a dozen aliases – *Arnold Chapman, Andrew Mason, Adam Rogers.* They were all listed in an old FBI file that I found on *microfiche.*

PAUL. What is this nonsense?!

   (*To* **MITCH.**) Mitch – GET HIM OUT OF HERE –

MIRANDA. *(To* **MITCH.**) NO – stay right where you are.

   (**PAUL** *turns to* **MIRANDA**, *as* **SAM** *continues –*)

SAM. All those names came in handy – *right, Arnold?* – since you had quite the record. Since *you were wanted in five states for wire fraud and extortion.*

PAUL.	**MIRANDA.**
How dare you come here and think you can –	Paul – what is this about?

SAM. But it's the name *Arnold Ratzlaff* that shows up on the hotel register. Not the electronic one – which is long gone, right Mitch? – no, it shows up on the *paper copy*, the one stored away in the hotel's archive.

CHELLE. He knows a guy.

SAM. Ten years ago – on the eighth of April – *Arnold Ratzlaff* checked into room five oh two of the Fairmont Hotel.

Three days later – after meeting a woman named Miranda Evans – he checked out of that hotel as *"Paul Rondine."*

Your wife never knew. But lucky for you, she launched a company that would give you exactly what you needed.

And the very first history you cleared was *your own*.

MIRANDA. *Paul...is that true?*

> *(A tense, charged beat – as they all stare at* **PAUL.***)*

PAUL. *(To* **MIRANDA.***) Of course it's not true.*

> *(To* **MITCH.***)* Mitch – lock it all down.

> *(To* **SAM***, a threat.)* No one is leaving.

MITCH. *(To* **SAM** *and* **CHELLE.***)* The gate is open.

PAUL. Mitch –

MITCH. Get out of here, Sammy –

PAUL. – no – goddamnit –

CHELLE. Goodnight, Mr. Ratzlaff.

> *(***CHELLE** *and* **SAM** *walk past* **MITCH** *and are gone.)*

(**MIRANDA** *is staring hard at* **PAUL,** *as* **PAUL**
turns and steps to the edge of the balcony –
staring offstage, as –)

(The sound of waves grows to a crescendo.)

19.

(Now.)

*(**CHELLE** and **SAM** at the park bench.)*

CHELLE. You could have told me you were coming there last night.

SAM. I know. I was worried I'd back away. Not go through with it.

CHELLE. You found everything. His whole history.

SAM. I found enough. And after we left –

(He stops.)

CHELLE. What?

(Beat.)

SAM. After we left, Paul was staring at the water.

Then, suddenly...without a word...he climbed over the railing...

And he was gone.

CHELLE. *(Quietly.)* Oh my god.

SAM. Mitch told me this morning.

"A father overcome by grief." That's what everyone will say.

CHELLE. And that's true.

That's completely true.

(They sit in silence for a moment.)

SAM. I asked Mitch: Why me? Out of all the guys at that coffee shop, I asked him – why'd you pick me?

He said: *"I don't know, Sam.*

SAM. *Why'd you say yes?"*

CHELLE. You had no idea what you were getting into.

But you dove in anyway.

I like that about you.

SAM. Chelle – listen...

CHELLE. Thank you for *seeing me.*

Really *seeing me.*

No one had ever done that before.

> (**CHELLE** *takes a paperback book out of her bag. She places it in* **SAM***'s hands.*)

This book is about a man and his friends who live in "A House Above the World."

Read it sometime.

And when you do...

Imagine me at the Mediterranean.

Imagine me floating in the sea.

> (**CHELLE** *kisses* **SAM** *on the cheek. Then she leaves.*)

> (**SAM** *watches...and watches...and watches her go. Then...*)

> (**SAM** *opens the book, as –*)

> (*Lights fade.*)

End of Play

www.ingramcontent.com/pod-product-compliance
Lightning Source LLC
Chambersburg PA
CBHW070351120726
47909CB00008B/2799